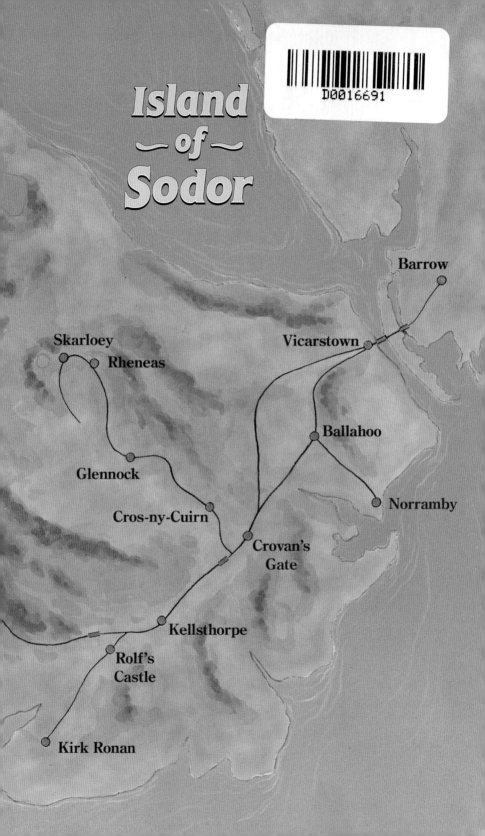

Thomas the Tank Engine & Friends™

CREATED BY BRITT ALLCROFT

Original holiday story based on The Railway Series by The Reverend W Awdry.
© 2010 Gullane (Thomas) LLC.
Thomas the Tank Engine & Friends and Thomas & Friends are trademarks of
Gullane (Thomas) Limited.
HIT and the HIT Entertainment logo are trademarks of HIT Entertainment Limited.

www.randomhouse.com/kids/thomas
www.thomasandfriends.com

Library of Congress Cataloging-in-Publication Data
Easter in Harwick / based on The Railway series by The Reverend W. Awdry ;
illustrated by Richard Courtney.
    p. cm.
"Thomas & Friends."
ISBN 978-0-375-85770-8 (alk. paper)
I. Awdry, W. II. Courtney, Richard, ill. III. Thomas the tank engine and friends.
PZ7.E126732 2010
[E]—dc22   2009019703

MANUFACTURED IN CHINA
10 9 8 7 6 5 4

HiT entertainment

Based on The Railway Series
by The Reverend W Awdry

Illustrated by Richard Courtney

RANDOM HOUSE 🏠 NEW YORK

Spring was springing everywhere Thomas went. Each day there were more buds on the trees and more flowers bursting from the ground. Thomas' riders were enjoying spring, too. Annie's and Clarabel's windows were open for the first time in a long while.

One morning, Sir Topham Hatt came into the Yard. "Thomas," he said, "I need Donald and Douglas for some heavy pulling at the harbor, and you will replace them in Harwick for a couple of days to keep things Right on Time up there."

"Yes, Sir," Thomas peeped. "That should be a fun adventure!"

Harwick is a town in the hilly countryside in the northernmost part of Sodor. As Thomas traveled north, Annie and Clarabel weren't carrying passengers, but were full of pretty straw baskets.

Harwick was chilly, but Thomas' Driver assured him it would be warming up soon. "The weather should be perfect for the big Easter egg hunt on Saturday."

"Egg hunt?" asked Thomas. "What can eggs hunt for?"

His Driver laughed. "Eggs don't do the hunting, Thomas. Children hunt for colored eggs that will be hidden in the town park. That's what the straw baskets are for—collecting eggs."

As promised, each day was warmer as Thomas chugged up and down the tracks around Harwick. And each day, Thomas would see Terence working hard, too. Terence's caterpillar treads helped him move around on the steep hills.

In a tree near the tracks, Thomas could see a pair of birds busily building a nest out of twigs and grass. One day, Thomas saw that the birds had found a piece of red ribbon, which gave the nest a cheery bit of color.

Now that nest reminds me of James, thought Thomas.

The day before the Easter egg hunt, Thomas saw Terence pulling a trailer full of eggs. The eggs had been dyed all the colors of the rainbow. Thomas had never seen eggs in so many colors.

Thomas waited for Terence as he drove down the muddy road.

As Terence easily turned the corner, he tooted a happy spring hello to Thomas. But the trailer didn't have caterpillar treads like Terence. The curve was sharp. The road was muddy. Oh, no!

The trailer slowly... slowly... slowly... rolled onto its side.

Hundreds of Easter eggs slipped off the trailer and rolled down the hill. They tumbled faster and faster down the grassy slope.

Some eggs got stopped by flowers and thick clumps of grass.

Some rolled to the edge of a stream.

A few eggs made it all the way to the fence around Farmer Dalby's garden.

"Oh, no!" cried Terence. "How are we ever going to get all of these eggs gathered and into town in time for the Easter egg hunt tomorrow?"

And then suddenly Thomas smiled. "I think I have an idea," he said.

The next morning, there were many children and their families at the town park. There was the big sign announcing the Easter egg hunt, but there were no baskets, and worse yet…there were no Easter eggs!

Just then Thomas pulled up.

Sir Topham Hatt was laughing and smiling.
"All aboard!" he cried. "All aboard for a quick trip
to the new Easter egg hunt location!"

And everyone happily boarded Annie and
Clarabel, who had been decorated just for the
special day.

Soon, everyone was heading out of Harwick towards Mr. Dalby's farm.

"If we cannot bring the Easter eggs to the children," peeped Thomas, "let's bring the children to the Easter eggs."

When they reached Dalby's Farm, all of the
children detrained and stood on the road, waiting
for the signal to begin.

Sir Topham Hatt started the big hunt.
"Ready…
Set…
Go!"

And the children were off. They looked
everywhere for the brightly colored Easter eggs.

They found the eggs in the bushes . . .

and by the stream.

Everyone was having fun.

Thomas and Sir Topham Hatt watched the children laughing and hunting.

Suddenly, Thomas noticed three blue eggs in a nest in a tree near the tracks. He was confused. "How did those eggs get up in that tree?" he asked. "Can Easter eggs fly?"

Sir Topham Hatt laughed. "Those aren't Easter eggs, Thomas. Those are robin's eggs. Soon they will hatch and be baby birds."

Thomas smiled and sighed. "Warmer weather, smiling children, Easter eggs, and baby birds... I can't wait for the rest of spring."

Can you find the following in the pictures of this story?